Mrs Pepperpot and the Hidden Treasure

A Red Fox Book

Published by Random House Children's Books
20 Vauxhall Bridge Road, London SW1V 2SA

A division of The Random House Group Ltd
London Melbourne Sydney Auckland Johannesburg
and agencies throughout the world

1 3 5 7 9 10 8 6 4 2

First published in Great Britain by
Hutchinson Children's Books 1987
Red Fox edition 1989
This Red Fox edition 2000

Printed in Singapore by Tien Wah Press (PTE) Ltd

The Random House Group Limited Reg. No. 954009

www.randomhouse.co.uk

ISBN 0 09 963790 1

Mrs Pepperpot and the Hidden Treasure

Alf Prøysen

Illustrated by David Arthur

RED
FOX

It was a fine sunny day in January, and Mrs Pepperpot was peeling potatoes at the kitchen sink.

'Miaow!' said the cat; she was lying in front of the stove.

'Miaow yourself!' answered Mrs Pepperpot.

'Miaow!' said the cat again.

Mrs Pepperpot suddenly remembered an old, old rhyme she learned when she was a child. It went like this:

The cat sat by the fire,
Her aches and pains were dire,
Such throbbing in my head,
She cried; I'll soon be dead!

Mrs Pepperpot stopped peeling potatoes, wiped her hands and knelt down beside the cat. 'There's something you want to tell me, isn't there, Puss? It's too bad I can't understand you except when I'm little, but it's not my fault.' She stroked the cat, but Puss didn't purr, she just went on looking at her.

'Well, I can't spend all day being sorry for you, my girl,' said Mrs Pepperpot, going back to the potatoes in the sink. When they were ready she put them in a saucepan of cold water on the stove, not forgetting a good pinch of salt. After that she laid the table, for her husband came home for his dinner at one o'clock and it was now half past twelve.

Puss was at the door now. 'Miaow!' she said, scratching at it.

'You want to get out, do you?' said Mrs Pepperpot, and opened the door. She followed the cat out, because she had noticed that her broom had fallen over in the snow. The door closed behind her.

And at that moment she shrank to her pepperpot size!

'About time too!' said the cat. 'I've been waiting for days for this to happen. Now don't let's waste any more time; jump on my back! We're setting off at once.'

Mrs Pepperpot didn't stop to ask where they were going; she climbed on Puss's back. 'Hold on tight!' said Puss, and bounded off down the little bank at the back of the house past Mrs Pepperpot's rubbish heap.

'We're coming to the first hindrance,' said Puss; 'just sit tight and don't say a word!' All Mrs Pepperpot could see was a single birch tree with a couple of magpies on it. True, the birds seemed as big as eagles to her now and the tree was like a mountain. But when the magpies started screeching she knew what the cat meant.

'There's the cat! There's the cat!' they screamed. 'Let's nip her tail! Let's pull her whiskers!' And they swooped down, skimming so close over Mrs Pepperpot's head she was nearly blown off the cat's back. But the cat took no notice at all, just kept steadily on down the hill, and the magpies soon tired of the game.

'That's that!' said the cat. 'The next thing we have to watch out for is being hit by snowballs. We have to cross the boys' playground now, so if any of them start aiming at you, duck behind my ears and hang on!'

Mrs Pepperpot looked at the boys; she knew them all, she had often given them sweets and biscuits. '*They* can't be dangerous,' she said to herself.

But then she heard one of them say: 'Here comes that stupid cat; let's see who can hit it first! Come on, Boys!' And they all started pelting snowballs as hard as they could.

The cat ran on till they got to a wire fence with a hole just big enough for her to wriggle through.

'So far, so good,' she said, 'but now comes the worst bit, because this is dog land, and we don't want to get caught. So keep your eyes open!'

The fence divided Mrs Pepperpot's land from her neighbour's, but she knew the neighbour's dog quite well; he had had many a bone and scraps from her and he was always very friendly. We'll be all right here, she thought.

But she was wrong. Without any warning, that dog suddenly came bearing down on them in great leaps and bounds! Mrs Pepperpot shook like a jelly when she saw his wide-open jaws all red, with sharp, white teeth glistening in a terrifying way.

She flattened herself on the cat's back and clung on for dear life, for Puss shot like a flash across the yard and straight under the neighbour's barn.

'Phew!' said the cat, 'that was a narrow squeak! Thanks very much for coming all this way with me; I'm afraid it wasn't a very comfortable journey.'

'That's all right,' said Mrs Pepperpot, 'but perhaps you'll tell me now what we've come for?'

'It's a surprise,' said Puss, 'but don't worry, you'll get your reward. All we have to do now is to find the hidden treasure, but that means crawling through the hay. So hang on!'

And off they went again, slowly this time, for it was difficult to make their way through the prickly stalks that seemed as big as beanpoles to Mrs Pepperpot.

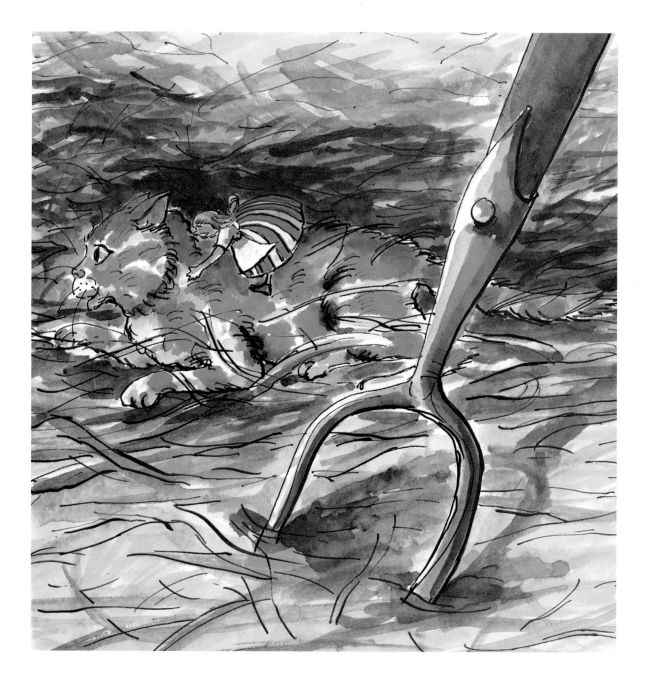

The dust was terrible; it went in her eyes, her mouth, her hair, down her neck – everywhere.

'Can you see anything?' asked the cat.

'Only blackness,' answered Mrs Pepperpot, 'and it seems to be getting blacker.'

'In that case we're probably going the right way,' said Puss, crawling further into the hay. 'D'you see anything now?' she asked.

'Nothing at all,' said Mrs Pepperpot, for by now her eyes were completely bunged up with hayseed and dust.

'Try rubbing your eyes,' said the cat, 'for this is where your hidden treasure is.'

So Mrs Pepperpot rubbed her eyes, blinked and rubbed again until at last she could open them properly.

When she did, she was astonished; all round her shone the most wonderful jewels! Diamonds, sapphires, emeralds – they glittered in every hue!

'There you are! Didn't I tell you I had a hidden treasure for you?' said the cat, but she didn't give Mrs Pepperpot time to have a closer look. 'We'll have to hurry back now, it's nearly time for your husband's dinner.'

So they crawled back through the hay and, just as they got out in the daylight, Mrs Pepperpot grew to her ordinary size. She picked the cat up in her arms and walked across the yard with her. The dog was there, but what a different dog! He nuzzled Mrs Pepperpot's skirt and wagged his tail in the friendliest way.

Through the gate they came to the place where
the boys were playing. Every one of them nodded
to her and politely said, 'Good morning'. Then they
went on up the hill, and there were the magpies in
the birch tree. But not a sound came from them;
they didn't even seem to notice them walking by.

When they got to the house Mrs Pepperpot put
the cat down and hurried indoors. It was almost
one o'clock. She snatched the saucepan from the
stove – a few potatoes had stuck to the bottom, so
she threw those out and emptied the rest into a
blue serving bowl. The saucepan she put outside
the back door with cold water in it.

She had only just got everything ready when Mr Pepperpot came in. He sniffed suspiciously. 'I can smell burnt potatoes,' he said.

'Nonsense,' said Mrs Pepperpot, 'I dropped a bit of potato skin on the stove, that's all. But I've aired the room since, so just you sit down and eat your dinner.'

'Aren't you having any?' asked her husband.

'Not just now,' answered Mrs Pepperpot, 'I have to go and fetch something first. I won't be long.'

And Mrs Pepperpot went back down the hill, through the gate to her neighbour's yard, and into the barn. But this time she climbed *over* the hay till she found the spot where her hidden treasure lay.

And what d'you think it was?

Four coal-black kittens with shining eyes!